The

LIGHTHOUSE FAMILY

W9-BJH-698

THE STORM

The

LIGHTHOUSE FAMILY

THE STORM

BY CYNTHIA RYLANT

ILLUSTRATED BY PRESTON MCDANIELS

SCHOLASTIC INC.

New York Toronto London Auckland Sydney
Mexico City New Delhi Hong Kong Buenos Aires

For Gracie, who loves the sea —C. R.
For Ruth, who gave me my sails —P. McD.

This book is a work of fiction. Any references to historical events, real people,
or real locales are used fictitiously. Other names, characters, places, and incidents are
the product of the author's imagination, and any resemblance to actual events or locales
or persons, living or dead, is entirely coincidental.

No part of this publication may be reproduced, stored in a retrieval system, or transmitted
in any form or by any means, electronic, mechanical, photocopying, recording, or otherwise,
without written permission of the publisher. For information regarding permission,
write to Aladdin Paperbacks, Simon & Schuster Children's Publishing Division,
1230 Avenue of the Americas, New York, NY 10020.

ISBN 0-439-80010-2

Text copyright © 2002 by Cynthia Rylant. Illustrations copyright © 2002 by Preston McDaniels.
All rights reserved. Published by Scholastic Inc., 557 Broadway, New York, NY 10012, by
arrangement with Aladdin Paperbacks, Simon & Schuster Children's Publishing Division.
SCHOLASTIC and associated logos are trademarks and/or
registered trademarks of Scholastic Inc.

12 11 10 9 8 7 6 5 4 3 2 1   5 6 7 8 9 10/0

Printed in the U.S.A.   40

First Scholastic printing, September 2005
The text of this book was set in Centaur.
The illustrations for this book were rendered in graphite.

Contents

I. *Pandora*

In a lonely lighthouse, far from city and town, far from the comfort of friends, lived a kindhearted cat named Pandora.

She had been living at this lighthouse all alone for four long years, and it was beginning to wear. She found herself sighing long, deep, lonely sighs. She sat on the rocks overlooking the waves far too long. Sometimes her nose got a sunburn.

And at night, when she tried to read by the lantern light, her mind wandered and she would think for hours on her childhood when she had friends and company.

Why did Pandora accept this lonely lighthouse life?

Because a lighthouse had once saved her.

When Pandora was but a kitten, she and her father had gone sailing aboard a grand schooner, bound for a new country. Pandora's mother had stayed behind, with the baby, to join them later.

And while they were at sea, Pandora and her father were shaken from their beds one night by an awful twisting of the ship's great bow.

"Stay here, Pandora!" her father had commanded. "Stay here and wait until I come for you!"

They were in a terrible storm. The wind was howling, and the waves crashed hard upon them. Worse, a deep fog had spread itself all over the water, and it is fog that will bring a ship to its end. Fog that will blind a sailor's eyes until his ship has hit the jagged shore and torn itself to pieces.

Pandora's father knew this as he strained with the others to keep the ship's sails aloft and his daughter trembled in her bed. He knew what somber danger they were in.

But Pandora's father was a brave cat and he would not give up hope. He would hold tight to the riggings with the others until help, in whatever form, might come to them.

In time, the winds began to settle and the waves grew smaller. But the dense fog refused to lift.

The ship's captain was clearly worried. For he knew these waters they sailed in. He knew the long history of ships gone down.

And he carried little hope that help might come to them, that someone might lead them away from the deadly shore. For only a lighthouse might show them the way, and there had been no working light on these waters for a hundred years.

So it was with much bewilderment, and amazement, and overwhelming *joy* that he heard, first, the deep, clear sound of a foghorn, then saw before him a *light*. Yes, a light! And it was not the light of another ship or small boat. Only a very powerful lamp could make itself seen through a fog like this. Only the lamp of a lighthouse.

"Pull leeward!" cried the captain. "Away from the light!"

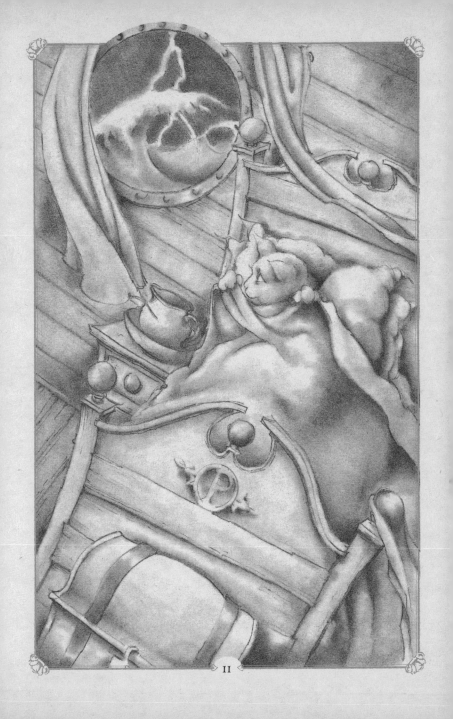

And everyone pulled hard on the riggings to make the ship turn, turn away from the dangerous shore.

The ship, and everyone on it, was saved.

Ever after, Pandora dreamed of lighthouses. Though she had not seen the beacon that had saved her, her father had, and he spoke of it often. He always wondered who had made the great light shine.

As she grew, Pandora herself came to think much on this. She went to the library and gathered books on lighthouses. She drew them in her sketch pad. She dreamed of them at night.

Then one morning she awoke and she knew what she must do. She must become a lighthouse keeper! She knew that this was her destiny.

It did not take Pandora long to find a lighthouse in need of keeping. It is a hard and lonely job, and few want it. Lighthouses are often built in unwelcoming places, atop sharp and dangerous rocks. A winter storm can hold a keeper inside for weeks on end. And when she finally emerges, there is no one to talk to. They are all someplace else, living in little towns or big cities. They are not interested in desolation.

But Pandora was not afraid of this life, for her heart was so good and clear that fear would not creep inside it. The ships in those unpredictable waters carried fathers and mothers and children, and they needed guiding. She knew she could do it.

And Pandora had been doing it, faithfully, for four long years. She had seen many an awful storm come and go. She had stayed awake long winter nights, tending the great lamp, sounding the deep horn.

Pandora did not know how many lives she had saved. But she knew that she had saved some.

And now, weary with being alone for so long, Pandora was about to save one more.

2. Seabold

There are those who love the sea so deeply, they cannot bear to be away from it even for a day. A dog named Seabold was one of these. He was born to a sailor's life.

When Seabold was old enough to leave home and family, he built himself a boat—which he named *Adventure*—said good-bye to his parents and sisters, and off he went, in search of the life meant for him.

He was a fine sailor. He had a keen understanding of the wind. He could read the stars. And he trusted his instincts.

For five years Seabold sailed the world's great oceans, and his instincts never failed him. He sailed safe and strong and free of worry.

But one day, this all changed.

Seabold had always known when a storm was coming. His nose told him so. And he had always found a sheltered cove or harbor in which to wait out the rough seas.

But this day, he had a cold. He had a cold and a stuffy nose, and his sense of smell was very bad. Added to this, he was tired. Seabold took a long, long nap in his bunk, and he did not notice the seabirds nervously circling in the air above him, agitated and calling to one another about the bad weather ahead.

The seabirds all wisely headed for land. But Seabold, adrift in his dreams, stayed out on open water.

Then the great storm hit.

Seabold was jolted from sleep by a sharp crack of lightning, a deep roar of thunder, and an enormous, crashing wave. As *Adventure* was flung here and there, up and down, Seabold clung to the little boat with all his strength, for there was nothing else he could do.

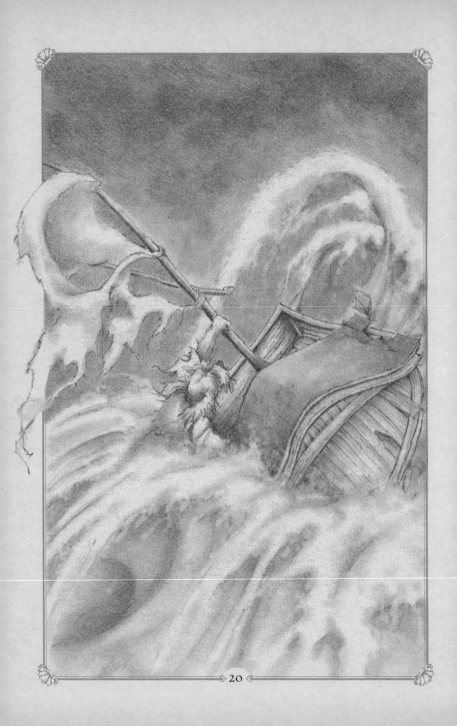

The sea, which had always been his friend, had turned against him. And for the first time in his sailor's life, Seabold was afraid.

He whispered into the wind, "Safe harbor. Let there be safe harbor."

Just as Seabold whispered these words, a magnificent light broke through the darkness, and the long, distant call of a horn sounded across the water.

"Safe harbor," Seabold repeated.

And this was the last thing brave Seabold said before he was lifted and rolled, over and over, into the deep black sea.

One might have thought the dog was forever lost.

But this is not the end of Seabold's story.

3. Comfort

When Seabold next awoke, he wondered if perhaps the storm had been just a dream.

For he found himself in a little wooden bed under a cheerful gingham quilt, and he was no longer *in* the sea, but looking out *at* the sea, through a small window by his side. A daisy stood in a jar on the windowsill.

Seabold tapped his head to be sure he wasn't dreaming. And just as he was about to try his legs on the shiny wooden floor, the door to his room opened and in stepped a cat.

She was smiling and had an apron tied around her waist. In her hands was a tray of tea and biscuits.

"Good morning," she said, setting the tray on the table beside the bed. "I hoped you might be awake. I am Pandora."

Still unsure whether he was dreaming, Seabold extended his paw to shake hers. "And I am Seabold," he said. "At least, I think I am."

Pandora smiled. "You have had a rather bad journey," she said.

"I thought it was my last," answered Seabold.

Pandora poured him a cup of tea, which smelled like flowers. Seabold drank it gratefully. "Thank you," he said. "May I have more? I'm so thirsty."

Pandora nodded and poured another cup. "All that salt water," she said.

"I don't know how I am alive," said Seabold.

"Nor do I," said Pandora. "When I found you on the shore three days ago, I was certain you were dead."

"I've been here three days?" exclaimed Seabold.

"Yes." Pandora smiled. "Sleeping like a baby."

Seabold shook his head. "I remember only going under," he said. "My boat—have you seen her?"

"Not yet," said Pandora. "But it may be farther down the shore. When you are able to walk, we shall go search."

"Able to walk?" said Seabold.

"Your leg," said Pandora.

Seabold drew back the gingham quilt. With surprise, he saw that his left leg was bandaged and splinted knee to foot. "Heavens," he said. "But, there is no pain. Shouldn't I be suffering?"

Pandora smiled with pleasure. "I am something of a doctor, I suppose," she said. "I have studied plants and learned those that heal. I wrapped your leg in plantain leaves to relieve the swelling. And the splint will prevent further injury."

"Amazing!" said Seabold.

Pandora blushed with pride.

"And are you alone here?" asked Seabold, sipping his tea. Pandora had poured herself a cup.

"Yes, all alone," she said. "Although I do have friends who stop by this island once in a while. In a *very* long while, I should say. They are seasonal."

"Seasonal?" said Seabold.

"They migrate," said Pandora. "So I see them only in spring and fall, as they make their way north or south. There is Atoll, the gray whale . . ."

"You know a whale personally?" asked Seabold.

"Oh yes," said Pandora. "Whales are very sociable once you break the ice. Ask them about their children and they'll go on forever."

"There is also Henry, the tern," she continued. "He's usually so pressed for time, he doesn't even land. He simply flutters above my head and asks after my health, my garden, and so forth. Then he's off. He flies six thousand miles every year."

"Really?" said Seabold.

"Yes," said Pandora. "He's quite fit."

"But you are alone nearly always?" asked Seabold.

"Nearly always," said Pandora.

Seabold shook his head. "I never thought I

would meet someone else like me," he said.

"Like you?" asked Pandora.

"One who loves the solitary life," said Seabold. "I am nearly always at sea, nearly always alone. Like you."

Pandora smiled and thought a moment. "I am not sure I *love* the solitary life," she said finally. "I simply live it."

"And why?" asked Seabold.

"To save lives," said Pandora. "Like yours."

And she poured him another cup of tea.

4. Companions

Everything at the lighthouse was different after Seabold's arrival.

Mornings when Pandora awoke, she remembered she had someone else to *talk* to. She leaped from bed and prepared a big breakfast of hot wheat cereal with cream, and apple scones, and bowls of huckleberries. She carried the tray to Seabold's room, and there they chatted all morning. Pandora's garden grew very weedy.

Then, once Seabold was able to hobble about on his leg with the help of a walking stick, their talks moved outside. Sitting on large rocks by the water, Pandora and Seabold told each other stories of their lives and things they had read or seen and what they liked most in this world or least.

Seabold told of his father, who feared the water and would not set foot in a boat.

Pandora told of her younger sister, who sewed wedding gowns for queens.

They both had read fairy tales as children and agreed that the bad animals were more interesting than the good ones.

And what did they like best in the world?

The northern lights, said Seabold.

Penguins, said Pandora.

Least, they both agreed, were shipwrecks.

It was summer, and Pandora's lighthouse responsibilities were small. For two months—July and August—there was little rain and hardly any fog. Ships traveled safely, and Pandora got a rest.

Well, somewhat. She still had to tend to preparing for the hard winter ahead. She knew she must grow and harvest vegetables, grind corn and wheat for bread, collect and cut driftwood for the fire. A supply boat had already delivered the year's kerosene for the lighthouse. All depended on Pandora being ready.

While Pandora gardened in the day, Seabold worked—as best he could, given his leg—on rebuilding his boat. He had indeed found it—at least, most of it—farther down the shore, and though his heart broke to see it so battered, he believed he could save it.

As Pandora gardened, she watched Seabold off in the distance tending to his boat, and she felt a small emptiness in her heart. The emptiness one feels watching a dear friend prepare to go away.

Evenings, the two made a picnic on the hill of daises leading to the shore and watched the sun go down, painting the world pink and red.

The next day, it all began again.

Seabold was very curious about the workings of the lighthouse, but his leg would not permit him to climb the four steep flights of stairs, then the ladder up into the lantern room to reach the great glass lamp. With no storms and no need for the saving lamp, Seabold sometimes forgot there was any lighthouse at all.

But one day in early September, just as the geese and the mallards and the warblers were beginning to fly overhead on their long journeys south, Seabold was awakened to exactly what that enormous lighthouse was meant to do.

And to just who was prepared to do it.

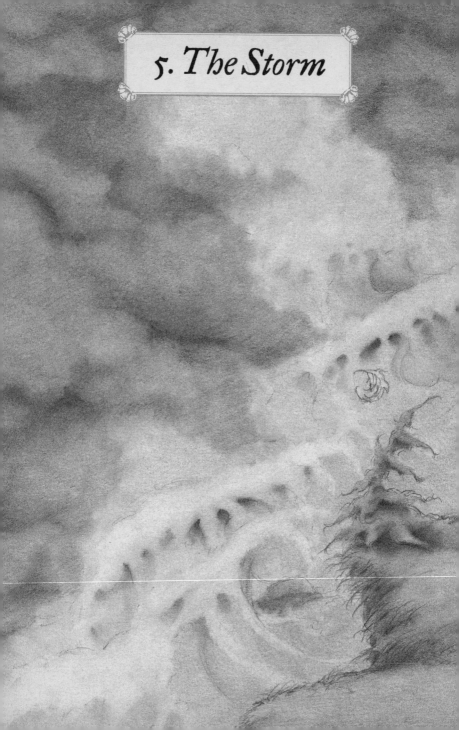

5. The Storm

It was much too early in the season, Pandora thought, for a storm to blow in. It was the season for fog, yes, but for serious ocean storms . . . those were due much later in the fall.

Then why, she wondered one afternoon in early September as she gathered tomatoes off the vines, was the sky growing so black? Why was the air so cold? Why were gulls circling higher and higher, their cries growing more and more frantic?

Because a sky above a sea loves unpredictability. It loves to surprise.

This day, it clearly intended to.

Seabold and Pandora battened down his boat, secured the shutters over the cottage windows, and set to building a fire in the kitchen stove.

"How cold it is!" said Seabold. "And yesterday was so warm."

"The sea is bringing us a different air," said Pandora. "One, I believe, full of danger. I must go up to the lantern room and attend to the light."

Seabold looked at his still-splinted leg in frustration. "I *have* to get up there to help you," he said.

"No, no," said Pandora. "Injury to your leg now will set you back a month of healing. Just keep the fire going while I work."

And while Seabold fed the fire in the kitchen and kept a pot of tea hot and ready for them both, Pandora climbed up to the lantern room. She trimmed the great lamp's wicks and lit them. She checked the kerosene vessel. She cleaned the storm panes. Then she climbed down to the watch room.

Just around suppertime, an enormous fog bank began rolling in. High in her tower, Pandora watched it spread toward land like creeping cotton, and she began to ring the bells and sound the horn that would guide smaller boats to shore, giving them escape from the storm that was surely about to hit.

Down in the kitchen, Seabold fretted. He listened to the bells and the horn. *I could be doing that,* he
thought. *I could be helping.* But he had to sit there by
the fire and wait. He was miserable.

Over the next few hours the wind built to an
astonishing speed, and its gusts rocked the tower
Pandora worked in. She was undaunted. It was
nightfall now, and this was a very bad storm for any
ship at sea. Fog, lightning, lashing rain, hard
wind—all could lead a ship onto the rocks and sink
her.

Pandora worked in the watch room, sounding
the horn again and again. Above her the great light
kept its strong beam out upon the water. She was
cold—she'd had no time to dress warmly or carry
wood to the watch room stove. But she could not
stop to remedy this. It was a terrible storm, and she
knew what a terrible storm could do.

In the kitchen, Seabold sat at the window and
watched the great light shine and listened to the

warning horn. One hour, two hours, three hours, four hours . . . How did Pandora do it? Where did she find the strength? He was only tending the kitchen fire and already he was tired.

Finally, sleep got the better of him. The storm raged on, without his witness.

Bright sun shining into the kitchen woke Seabold the next morning. He had lain beside the stove all night. And where was Pandora? He looked out the window.

And there she was, far out near the edge of a cliff, a shawl about her shoulders and her paw in the air, waving.

Off in the water, barely a spot on the horizon, was a sailing ship. At rest. Safe.

She saved them, thought Seabold.

He watched his friend in wonder.

6. Purpose

Seabold had planned to sail away by October's end, before the hard winter storms began, before the ice and wind. He was a sailing dog, the sea was his home. He knew this and Pandora knew this, and they both were prepared for the sorrowful good-bye.

But destiny had other plans.

Seabold's boat did not come together as quickly as he'd hoped. Small essential pieces were still missing and had to be made by hand. This would take time. It would take a long spring and a long summer and perhaps an entire fall as well.

Seabold was resourceful. But he could not invent time.

And his leg was very slow in healing. It had been

a bad break, and in spite of Pandora's marvelous herbs and capable splinting, the leg was weak. Seabold still walked with the aid of a stick.

Thus, as the wind grew crisper and harder and the sky filled with birds going away, Seabold stood at the edge of the shore and realized that this winter he would not sail.

He thought that he would be despondent. He thought that he would be depressed.

But he wasn't.

Something had happened to him as he watched the noble efforts of Pandora save others, to serve a purpose higher than herself.

Seabold had been inspired. And he thought that perhaps, at least for one winter, he might also make his life count for something.

So he asked if he might stay on till spring.

And, of course, she said yes. It had been her secret wish.

Together they gathered wood for winter fires and food for winter sustenance. And Seabold was finally able to climb all the way up to the great lamp. He was astonished, seeing it for the first time. "It is magnificent!" he said to Pandora. "It is a wonder!"

Seabold and Pandora polished the brass fittings of the great lamp. They disassembled and cleaned the lanterns. They replaced worn wicks. Being in the lantern room thrilled Seabold as much as even the finest sailing day. (Though he would not admit this to Pandora.)

And in the evenings, as Pandora knit warm caps and mittens and socks for them both, and as Seabold fashioned tools from driftwood, they talked.

"I am astonished," said Seabold one night, "that I am not land-sick by this time. I have never before been able to stay ashore so long without feeling my legs turn to stone."

Pandora smiled and shifted the cap she was knitting for him. "I hope you will not be too unhappy with this lonely lighthouse life," she said.

"Oh no," said Seabold. "I am quite looking forward to it. I am hoping to be useful."

"And you shall be," said Pandora.

"I hope we will meet new friends," said Seabold, "as the days go by. Even if they are only passing through. I should like very much to know a whale."

"The sea is full of surprises," said Pandora. "New friends among them."

She looked at Seabold with a twinkle. "I should know," she said.

"In spring," said Seabold, "before I finish the work on *Adventure*, I will build a gazebo at the top of the daisy-hill. And from there we may sit and see what comes our way."

"Oh," answered Pandora, "many wonderful things. There shall be many wonderful things."

She added another log to the fire.

They both felt wonderfully warm.

7. The Rescue

The winter was long indeed. Seabold had always spent the colder months sailing in sunny climes. He had nearly forgotten what it was to have frosty toes.

In Pandora's lighthouse, from November to March, he was reminded every single day.

In the worst of the cold days, the entire island was covered with ice. The spray from the sea washed over every piece of ground, every bush, every rock, and it froze solid. Pandora and Seabold did not venture out for weeks at a time.

It was just as well, for the storms were furious. Seabold and Pandora were needed day and night at the lamp. Day and night they tended the mantle and shone their beacon of warning across the water.

If they saved lives, they did not know whose, or when. And if anyone out in the gray waters sent them a prayer of thanks, they did not know it. They did not hear it.

Still, when finally the exhausted cat and dog laid their heads down to a brief sleep, they slept well, and with contented hearts.

Spring was never quite sure when She was arriving. One day the sky would be a clear, brilliant blue and the sun would shine its head on the small white crocuses around Pandora's door. Then the next day a wind would roar in like a hurricane and rain would bend all the new flowers to the ground and set everything a-shiver.

Seabold made several false starts on his gazebo before the sun finally came out and stayed out long enough for a soul to get some work done.

And it was while he was hammering on the gazebo atop the daisy-hill that Seabold saw what looked to be a floating crate far out upon the water. And above it what looked to be a small flag.

Seabold did not yet know it, but something wonderful was about to happen to Pandora's lonely lighthouse.

"Pandora!" Seabold cried. "Come and look!"

From behind the cottage, Pandora emerged with an armload of firewood. She set the wood by the door and hurried to the top of the hill.

"Look," said Seabold. He pointed toward the water where the crate floated. He could see no signs of life.

"It has some sort of flag," he told Pandora. "Do you think it is empty?"

Pandora gazed out across the water, and her face grew very serious. "I have a feeling," she said soberly. "I believe there is life out there."

Seabold frowned. "Well, if life *is* out there," he answered, "it is not at all well, you may be certain of that. For that crate is surely drifting at the mercy of the sea."

Pandora nodded. "I know," she said.

Seabold took a deep breath and straightened his

shoulders. "I shall just have to go fetch it to shore," he said.

Pandora looked at him. "And how will you do that?" she asked.

"I think I can manage my boat out that far," said Seabold. "She's torn, but I think she will float."

"You *think?*" repeated Pandora.

"We can stand here and watch that small flag float away and goodness-knows-what tragedy with it," said Seabold. "Or I can make *Adventure* float."

Pandora sighed deeply, but with resolve. "Make her float," she said. "And be quick."

Seabold ran toward the shore.

8. Children

It did not take long for the brave dog to get his tattered boat upon the water, or to reach the drifting crate. He was, after all, still a very fine sailor.

"Hello!" he called as he steered nearer. He could see that the flag was actually a small red shirt on a stick. "Anyone there?"

Silence.

Gravely, he pulled his boat alongside, expecting the worst.

He peered inside. "My *goodness*," he said.

For there, peering back at him, were three very young mice. One, in fact, was a baby. All three were piled close together.

"Are you injured?" asked Seabold.

One of the mice, the boy, opened his mouth to

speak, but no sound came out. The girl-mouse simply stared. The baby was asleep.

"Are you lost?" asked Seabold.

The boy-mouse and the girl-mouse nodded vigorously.

Seabold extended his paw. "You must come with me, children," he said. "For your situation is very bad."

Nodding her head in agreement, the girl-mouse reached out for his paw. He lifted her aboard. Then the boy-mouse gently handed him the baby. She was so small and light that Seabold barely breathed as he carefully placed her in the lap of the older mouse.

"Is the baby your sister?" he asked the girl-mouse.

Yes, she nodded.

Finally the boy-mouse was on board, still unable to speak.

Seabold quickly turned back toward shore. "Thirst has gotten the better of you," he said. "We must get you to fresh water and fast."

When Seabold carried all three to shore, in his knitted cap, Pandora was there, waiting with a blanket and—blessedly—a bowl of water. The children drank and drank. The girl-mouse made a cup of her hand for the baby.

When they had finished drinking, the boy-mouse said, quite clearly and solemnly, "Thank you."

Seabold and Pandora smiled. For both were, deep down inside themselves, quite delighted. *Children!*

They took the little ones into the cottage and gave them supper.

The next morning the boy-mouse and girl-mouse joined Pandora and Seabold at breakfast. The evening before they had introduced themselves as Whistler and Lila, brother and sister. The baby they had introduced as Tiny.

"Yes indeed, she is," Pandora had replied.

"No, no," Lila had said. "Tiny is her proper name."

"Well," Pandora had replied with a smile. "Perfect."

And now, in early morning, sitting before a warm breakfast in a warm kitchen, Whistler and Lila, still tired, still hungry, were, more than anything, *worried*.

"Tiny is still sleeping," Lila told Pandora and Seabold. "She never sleeps so long."

"And she hardly stirred all night," said Whistler. "She always stirs about and gurgles and bubbles. But she is so quiet."

Pandora rose immediately to see.

She lifted the sleeping baby from the knitted sock on the chair.

"This small one has a fever," Pandora said in deep concern. "I believe she is quite ill."

Lila gazed at Pandora, and one large tear began to roll down the small mouse's face.

Whistler looked at Seabold in distress.

"Seabold," said Pandora, "you will need to look after this baby while I go out into the woods. I must find a special branch of willow, and it may take me some time."

Seabold nodded and reached out. Pandora gently laid the infant in his big paw.

"Keep her cool," said Pandora. "But not cold. A nice, low breeze from the window will help. And she needs much water. See if she will drink."

Pandora looked kindly at Whistler and Lila. "You have done very well, caring for this small child. She is ill from weather and sea, not from want of attention or love."

Another tear dropped down Lila's face.

"I shall hurry," Pandora said as, taking her woolen shawl, she stepped out the door.

9. Family

While Pandora went out searching the woods, Seabold sat Lila and Whistler down to a checkerboard he had made, to take their minds off their fears.

"I will look after Tiny," he told them gently. "And you may try out my new game board."

"Clams!" Lila said in surprise, picking up a game piece.

"And starfish," said Whistler, picking up another.

Seabold smiled. "They're much more interesting than little round circles. I carved them myself."

"Amazing," said Whistler, turning the starfish in his hand. "I should like to try carving sometime."

"Anytime you like," said Seabold. "Except just now, of course. This little one needs me."

He left Whistler and Lila to their game and carried the infant-mouse to a chair beside the kitchen window. Settling her in one paw, with a thimbleful of water nearby, he went about his duties.

Keep her cool, Pandora had told him. Give her water.

And these things Seabold did do.

But he did something more.

There, beside Pandora's gingham-curtained window, in view of the cherry trees budding and the daffodils in bloom, Seabold transformed.

Exactly how, he could not say. But rocking the infant carefully in his paw, listening to the quiet and gentle voices of Whistler and Lila in the next room, hearing the fire crackle and smelling the good brown smell of bread in the stove, Seabold realized that he was happy. Happier than he had ever been. Happier than any solitary evening at sea had ever made him.

He sat by the window, cooed to the tiny baby, and smiled.

And after that day, *everything* was changed.

Tiny was made better by the willow bark. Lila planted sunflower seeds. And Pandora and Seabold found themselves with a kind of *household.* Some days Pandora looked about at all the dwellers at her lighthouse and she marveled. *How had it all happened?*

It had happened for many reasons. It happened because a noble young cat wished to save lives. Because a brave dog wished to sail. And because three small children wished for a family.

Before Seabold found them at sea, Whistler, Lila, and Tiny had lived in an orphanage far from Pandora's lighthouse. But they were to be separated and sent off to different places. "We will *never* be separated," Whistler had told Lila. And in the dark of night, with Tiny bundled onto Lila's back, they had escaped.

Finding the docks of the city, and all the great schooners ready to set sail, they had hidden aboard one of them, bound for they knew not where.

But out at sea, in a hurricane wind, the schooner

had rolled itself under and the three poor young mice with it.

Perhaps their parents in heaven were watching over them. For Whistler managed to grab hold of an empty crate and pull his sisters in.

They floated, hungry and thirsty, for what seemed time unending, until Seabold found them.

And now here they were, carving otters, planting sunflowers.

Seabold grew quite attached to Tiny. He put her in the soft roll of his knitted cap and she went everywhere with him, seeing all that he saw.

In evening, when Pandora set supper on the table, Seabold placed Tiny in a little eggcup by his plate and patted her fondly on the head as they ate.

And when, with full stomachs and happy hearts, the children were put to bed, Seabold and Pandora had their last cup of tea in the sitting room and reminisced.

"Do you remember when we saw the double rainbow?"

"Do you remember when the moon passed across the sun?"

"And the wind blew the pelican the wrong way?"

They would smile together in memory and sip their tea.

And, as always, before the night was ended, Seabold would ask, "And do you remember when I found the children?"

Pandora would nod her head.

"They are quite wonderful," Seabold would say.

"Yes," Pandora would answer.

"Thank goodness we found them," both would say in unison.

And with a happy good night, Seabold would go to his warm bed and Pandora would go to hers. In the kitchen, near the fire, tucked into the knitted sock Pandora had made just for them, the three mouse-children would sleep soundly, dreaming their blue sea dreams.

The lighthouse had a family.

The Beginning